THE NORTH POLE MYSTERY

WRITTEN BY MARY BLOUNT CHRISTIAN
ILLUSTRATED BY JOE BODDY

Milliken Publishing Company, St. Louis, Missouri

Cover Design by Henning Design, St. Louis, Missouri

Library of Congress Catalog Card Number: 88-60633
ISBN 0-88335-597-3 (pbk.)/ISBN 0-88335-593-0 (lib. bdg.)

David Cooper was sitting on his front steps.
His friends Ann and Walter came up.
"What are you doing?" Ann asked him.

"I'm reading my new book," David said.
"And I'm watching Adam for Mother."

"That's funny," Walter said.
"I see your book, but I don't see Adam."

David laid down his book.
"He was here a minute ago.
Adam!" he called. "Where are you?"
There was no answer.

"Maybe he went into the house," Ann said.

1

David went inside.
He looked in each room.
Adam was not in the house.

Next, David ran outside.
"Adam!" David called.

Pedro came over. "What's up?" he asked.

"Adam is gone," David said. "He is a pest.
But I love my little brother. I'm afraid.
Where can he be? I'll look in the backyard."

2

"I'll look down Sherlock Street," Walter said.

"I'll look up Sherlock Street," Ann said.

"And I'll look across Sherlock Street," Pedro said.

The four children ran off.
"Adam!" they called.
There was no answer.

3

Later the children went
back to David's house.
"I have an idea," Walter said.
"I'll call my dog, Watson.
Watson can find Adam."

Ann laughed. "Watson cannot find his own tail!"

Walter's face turned red. "Just you wait!
You will see! Watson will help us find Adam."

Pedro looked up. "The sun is behind the trees,"
he said. "It will be dark in a few hours."

"Get Watson, Walter," David said.
"Maybe he can help us find Adam."

"Here, Watson!" Walter called.
"Come here, Watson."

Watson ran to Walter.
"Woof! Woof!" he said.

"Good dog, Watson," Walter said.
"Go find Adam." Watson sat down.

"No, Watson," Walter said.
"Adam. Find Adam."
Watson rolled over.

"Your dog cannot find Adam,"
David said. "What can we do?
I should have watched Adam.
I should have played with him,
but I read my book instead."
David put his head in his hands.
Ann put her hand on his shoulder.

"Don't worry, David," she said.
"We will find him."

Walter kept a notebook in his pocket.
He pulled it out. He pulled out his pencil too.
"When did you last see Adam?" Walter asked.

"What a good idea!" Pedro said.
"Walter can write all the clues
in his notebook."

"When we have all the clues,
we will find Adam," Ann said.

Watson stood on his back legs.
"Woof! Woof!" he said.

"Stop that, Watson," Walter said.
"We have to think about clues.
First, when did Adam leave?"

"I don't know," David said.

"What did Adam have on?" Walter asked.

"That does not matter," Ann said.
"We know he is gone.
And we know what he looks like.
What we need to know is what
you were doing before he left."

"Adam wanted to go for a walk,"
David said. "I didn't want to go.
I tried to make him think about something else.
I showed him my compass.
I told him it was like magic.
I showed him how the needle
always points toward the North Pole.
Adam said the compass pointed to Santa's house.
He loves to hear about Santa."

David looked around. "My compass is gone!
Adam must have it."

Walter wrote in his notebook:

1. Adam wanted to go for a walk.
2. Compass missing.
3. Compass points to North Pole
4. Adam loves to hear about Santa

"I think Adam has gone for a walk," Walter said.
"And I think he needed your compass to get where he wanted to go."

Ann clapped her hands.
"Adam is walking to the North Pole!
He is following the compass needle!"

"Then we must follow a compass needle too," Pedro said.
"Does anyone have a compass?"

Everyone said no.

"Then we will have to make one," Pedro said.
"We need a magnet with the ends marked *N* and *S*,
a thin piece of cork, a plastic bowl,
a needle, and some glue."

The children got the things they needed.
Pedro filled the bowl with water.

"Now I must magnetize the needle," he said.
Pedro put the needle on the ground.
He stroked the needle with the *S* end of the magnet.
He did not move the magnet back and forth on the needle.
He started at the eye of the needle each time
and moved across to the point.
He stroked the needle about fifty times.
"Now it should be magnetized," he said.

Pedro glued the needle onto the cork.
Then he put the cork into the water.
The needle turned in the water and then stopped.
"The sharp end of this magnetized needle
is pointing to the north,"
Pedro told his friends.

The children walked to
where the needle pointed.
They went down David's driveway.
They went past the garage.
They went past the tree house.
They went right to the back fence!

"Adam cannot get over this fence," David said.
"It is too tall."

"Woof! Woof!" Watson said.

Ann laughed and pointed.
"Look at that silly dog!
Now he is barking at a tree!"

Watson stood on his back legs.
He put his front paws on the tree.
"Woof! Woof!" he said.

"He is not barking at the tree," Walter said.
"He is barking at something *in* the tree.
And I think I know what it is!"

25

Walter went up the tree.
Ann, David, and Pedro went up too.

There in the tree house they found Adam sound asleep.
He still had David's compass in his hand.

"Adam, wake up!" David said.
He put his arms around Adam.
"I'm so glad you are all right."

"I was going to the North Pole without you," Adam said.

"This isn't the North Pole," David said.

"I know," Adam said.
"But I couldn't really go there.
Mother won't let me cross the street by myself."

David laughed. "I'm glad.
Let's go into the house.
It's time to eat."

"Thank you for your help," David told his friends.

"Woof! Woof!" Watson said.

"Thank you too, Watson," David said.

Walter put his notebook away.
"We are very good detectives," he said.
"We should call ourselves the
Sherlock Street Detectives."

"Yes!" the others said.

"Woof! Woof!"

"Yes, you too, Watson," Walter said.

Watson rolled over on his back.

"Woof! Woof!"

Glossary

compass – Something used to show which way north, south, east, and west are. The needle on a compass points to the north.

cork – The outer part of some oak trees. Pieces of cork are pushed into the tops of some bottles to close them.

eye – The hole in a sewing needle.

magnet – A piece of rock or metal that pulls iron or steel toward it.

magnetize – To make something act like a magnet.

needle – The pointer on a compass.

North Pole – The place on earth that is the farthest north.

Vocabulary

across	cross	front	magnetized	plastic	stood
Adam	dark	garage	marked	pocket	street
afraid	David Cooper	glue	matter	point(s)	stroked
Ann	detectives	glued	minute	pointed	tail
answer	driveway	gone	move	pointing	thank
anyone	else	ground	moved	pulled	thin
arms	everyone	head	needle	really	things
around	eye	hear	next	right	toward
backyard	face	hours	north	rolled	tried
barking	fence	idea	North Pole	Santa	turned
behind	few	instead	notebook	sharp	wake
bowl	fifty	kept	others	Sherlock	Walter
brother	filled	know	ourselves	shoulder	watched
children	first	laid	paws	silly	watching
clapped	follow	laughed	Pedro	something	water
clues	following	leave	pencil	sound	Watson
compass	forth	magic	pest	started	won't
cork	found	magnet	piece	steps	worry
couldn't	friends	magnetize			